Ink for the unsaid

Adam Sheppard

This is a work of creative nonfiction and poetry. Names, events, and experiences are presented as truthfully as possible from the author's perspective. Any similarities to persons living or deceased, beyond those specifically mentioned, are coincidental.

Certain sections reference military experiences, including those associated with the United States Marine Corps. These reflections are the personal views of the author and do not represent official policies or positions of the United States Government or the Department of Defense.

Scripture references, if any, are taken from the Holy Bible.

Book Title: Ink for the Unsaid
Author: **Adam Sheppard**

First Edition

ISBN: 979-8-89571-337-2

Cover design and interior layout by: Gloriana Adeyeye

Printed in the United States of America

Dedication & Thanks

Above all, I am thankful to God, for blessing me with the talent to put these thoughts and words together. To my father, Lionel Sheppard, and to my late mother, Lori Brooks (Sheppard), for the life that inspired the works within the pages.

This book would also not be possible without the encouragement of my sophomore English teacher, Mrs. Black, for her kindness, encouragement of my early talent, and her belief in me.

I owe a special thanks to Kim Dillon, for teaching me the power of forgiveness, Chad Scoggins for teaching me the proper way to forgive, and Yorbe Caoba, my life coach, thank you all for giving me my life back.

To Brandon, Allyson, and Brody Hyatt for your genuine friendship and true meaning of family you have shown me. To Curt Moreno, for reminding me that I am a warrior, and fighting back-to-back with me thru one of the toughest battles. To Mr. James "Jimmy" Lodge, for a father's love; and for being everything you were, and teaching me everything you could. Rest in peace, my dear friend. To Paul Gulsvig, for the education, inspiration, the music, and for the dream.

To California's Yuba River, and to my brother Chase, for taking me to experience the magical healing there. To Colorado and the Conejos, that breathed into me new life, and helped me to heal my body, mind, heart, and soul.

To my fellow warriors: veterans, first responders of all services, Semper Fi!

And finally, this book is dedicated to the reader. May you find your own "Yuba and Conejos" that brings you happiness, and the peace that passes understanding on this life journey we all share.

-A

Contents

Dedication & Thanks	iii
Contents	iv
The Talent	3
Is There a Santa Claus?	5
Dream Date	7
Desires of a Young Heart	9
Get On the Line	11
The Country Life Way	13
Service & Duty	17
James "Mr. Jimmy" Lodge	22
What's In a Name	25
Rivers of Life	29
The Water & the Woodlands	32
Lessons	35
My Life Coach	39
A Year of Change	45
Rodney's Cowboy Hat	49

I started my freshman year of high school Wednesday, August 23, 1995. My family was very involved in church growing up, and I had a crush that I had been wanting to ask on a date. Her name was Bethany Anne Spurlin. She had an older brother named Paul, and a cousin named David that I held in high esteem.

I wasn't sure what she would say, but I liked her because she sang like an angel, and I too was very much into the singing part of church and the youth devotional songs we sang at the youth devotional gatherings. She was a few years older than me, but I decided the Sunday night prior that I would somehow muster the courage to talk to her at the upcoming Wednesday service, which happened to be my first day of High School.

As I got into the car that afternoon after school, my mother's energy was off, and she told my brother and I that Bethany had been killed in a bad car accident that very morning. I didn't say anything. I couldn't believe what I was hearing.

During that same school year, my high school lost three people, one teacher and two students. The students were killed in car accidents and the teacher passed away from natural causes.

This was the beginning of my poetry writing, and the poem below is one of my first works.

The Talent

Sometimes it takes just one event,
To turn your life around;
And in the midst of all the chaos,
A new talent can be found.

And if they had not been killed last year,
And gone to God above;
Then I would not have discovered,
This talent which I love.

It's from their deaths I prospered,
And I'll never be the same,
Because of the talent recognized,
When people say my name.

And I thank God for this talent
That I discovered and now know,
And I now thank them for helping me,
Discover it a year ago.

Is There a Santa Claus?

I wrote the poem you are about to read in my sophomore year of High School.

I had English as my first period class, and each day our teacher, Mrs. Black, would put a journal topic on the board for us to write about. These journals were a part of our grade every six weeks, so it was mandatory that we participated. Some days, the topic simply said, "Free Write", which meant we could scribble anything that was on our minds. However, on this particular day, being that the Christmas holiday was around the corner, the topic stated, "Is there a Santa Claus?" Having recently been exposed to the movie, "Yes, Virginia, There Is a Santa Claus" I decided that it would be fun to write a poem in the same tenor that the letter to little Virginia O'Hanlon received from Santa himself in her local newspaper.

When my teacher read this poem, she asked me to write another copy so that she could display it on her wall, which I did.

I felt flattered that she thought enough of this little poem to want to put it on her bulletin board for all the students she had throughout the day to enjoy.

Is There a Santa Claus?

As long as children
Kneel to pray,
Beside the bed
In which they lay;

And as long as parents
Dare to say,
"Hurry! To Bed!
Santa's on his way!"

As long as the legend lives
And the story is always told,
And the children write "Dear Santa,"
With a pen that's deep and bold;

And as long as
Bells jingle,
And kids hear
Of Kris Kringle,

Yes, there is,
And will always be,
A Santa Bringing happiness
To you and to me.

Dream Date

My sophomore English teacher, Mrs. Black, used to always come up with the most interesting journal entry topics; and when this one came up, I suppose I just let my imagination go, and I came up with this creative little poem as I fantasized about what a perfect date would look like for me, in my own perfect world. Since the Valentine's holiday was just a few days away, the subject had to be a journal entry. Being an avid outdoorsman who loved spending time on the water as much as in the woods, this poem seemed fitting to me for a perfect date at the time.

Dream Date

My dream date
Would have to be,
With someone special
And close to me.

We'd row through a lake
Like in a quiet dream;
The sky would be blue
And the stars would gleam.

The midnight sky
Would be quite clear,
As I'd lean and whisper
In her ear.

I'd hold her tight
And kiss her lips;
Then caress her face
With my fingertips.

I'd hold her silky hand in mine
As I sing her favorite song;
And hope the night would never die,
But wish it would live on.

The night would finally have to end
By becoming a brand-new day;
And I'd take her home, not as my friend,
But as my fiancé.

 # Desires of a Young Heart

While in High School, I was honored to audition for, and be accepted to, the Alabama All-State Choir in the second half of my sophomore year. The students selected traveled to Auburn University for an intense singing camp for almost a week, followed by a performance in the University's theatre for the families and paying attendees.

Our music instructor for the Alabama All-State Choir at Auburn University was a man named Paul Gulsvig. He is a truly inspirational man that had a profound impact on my life. On one of the first days of our camp, he gave all of us an incredibly inspiring work that he had written about what he desired his life to be. I still have my autographed copy to this day, and still read it periodically. His words, and the way in which he delivered them were unlike anything else that I'd ever read, and had impacted me so strongly to that point in my life.

The work you are about to read is my own attempt to put into words the things I desired most at that time in my youth; after Mr. Gulsvig had such an impact on my way of thinking and articulating my own desires, for the life which I hoped I was destined to live.

Desires of a Young Heart

Give me my name whispered on the wind,
Give me the love that will never end.
Give me plenty of moments of bliss,
Give me the soft, silky rose's kiss.
Give me courage and give me power,
Give me more knowledge and wisdom each hour.
Give me the stars in a midnight sky,
Give me a lover with sparkling eyes.
Give me some time to pray all alone,
Give me a beautiful Heavenly home.
Give me a seat on God's right hand,
Give me a place in Heaven to stand.
Give me sweet honey, made by the bees,
Give me the year-round evergreen trees.
Give me the seasons: winter, spring, summer, fall;
Give me the pleasure that goes with them all.
Give me time for endless days,
Give me happiness, joy, and play.
Give me a chance to undo mistakes,
Give me a moment to end a heartache.
Give me a chance to un-break a heart,
Give me just one good reason to start.
Give me every ocean blue,
Give me this life until mine is through.

Get On the Line

One of the most memorable things about Marine Corps boot camp are the drill instructors counting down the seconds to zero. During these countdowns, usually from ten, the recruits are instructed to yell "GET ON THE LINE!!!", when the count reaches a certain number. For our platoon, it was number three. Every time a drill instructor hit 'three' we all chorused in unison, "GET ON THE LINE!!!" as loud as we could, while making the mad dash in desperation to arrive at our respective places on "the line" and be at the position of attention before the count reached one.

The following poem is a humorous bit I wrote as I was thinking about how great it was going to be to graduate Marine Corps boot camp from Parris Island, South Carolina just two days later.

Semper Fi

Get On the Line

The lights come on
At Zero-Five
"Get outta the rack
And get your ass on line!"

"Hurry up and get dressed;
Those boots better shine
And when your rack is made
Get your ass on line!"

"Get out, line up
That chow smells fine;
So if you're hungry boys
Get your ass on line!"

"Form it up for haircuts,
Yes, again it's time,
Tuck in those collars
Get your ass on line!"

"Graduation is here
It's about Damn Time,
So get your shit packed up
And get your ass on line!"

"Take your bags boys
Get 'em on outside,
You want to leave this place,
Get your ass on line!"

"Marine, take your orders
And at this time,
You get to leave this island,
Get your ass OFF line!"

 # The Country Life Way

I wrote this poem one day as I was thinking about my childhood and my grandparents' home, reeling back the years living in the country, when things were so much simpler. I could write pages of stories about all the adventures on that land in the foothills of the Appalachians where my grandparents' home was nestled.

I have an immense amount of gratitude for the mountains, ponds, creeks, pastures and all the other country resources that I was blessed with growing up in north Alabama.

I hope this work paints a picture of my early life as I experienced it. There really is nothing comparable to growing up with the grandparents that I had. Their 85-acre farm and all that went with it; the work, the hunting, the fishing, camping, growing gardens and raising animals; participating in life and death, was significant in formulating my outlook of the world, and my place in it.

My memories of the farm are fond, and my love of the place and the people who made that parcel of land so incredibly special remains. Now that it is gone, along with the people that made it so very special, the memories are all that's left.

This poem is one of my personal favorites of all of my writings, and I hope you can live vicariously through me as you enjoy it.

I only wish everyone could experience The Country Life Way, if only for a moment.

The Country Life Way

As life fleets along
And the seasons go by,
I sit back and watch them,
And inhale a deep sigh.

The warmth of Spring comes
With feelings of love;
The Dogwood trees bloom
With rain from above.

The leaves all turn green
And the grass starts to grow;
The park comes alive,
Children swing to and fro.

And then comes the Summer
With hot endless days;
Grilled burgers and dogs
At my grandparents' place.

By the time darkness comes
We're still not in bed;
We're out on the lawn
Catching Fireflies instead.

And then with the Fall
The leaves start to change;
The weather turns cool,
And we get some good rain.

The days go by quickly;
It gets dark too soon,
But not much compares
To Fall nights with full moons.

Next comes the Winter,
The temperature; cold,
But country sky stars
Still shine bright and bold.

Christmas at Grandpa's
Brings smoked juicy ham,

Macaroni and cheese,
Pecan pie and yams.

The kids open gifts
Then the men have their fun;
They all go outside
And shoot their new guns.

Late in the day
The women go for a walk,
While the men eat some cookies
And have a long talk.

The seasons go by
As I live day by day,
And I love nothing more,
Than the country life way.

About Service & Duty

I am thankful and grateful to the men and women who have served the United States of America. Across all continents, and in theatres across the globe, the brave individuals who choose "service and duty", and "we, over me" are an integral part of the freedoms we enjoy in the United States and take for granted every day.

Often the sacrifices they make are unnoticed, uncelebrated, unreported, underrated, underpaid, and unappreciated.

I appreciate my fellow brothers and sisters in arms.

God Bless you all.

God Bless America.

This poem is simply a story. Any and all similarities to actual events in recent or distant history are purely coincidental.

No children or pets were harmed in the writing of this poem.

Service & Duty

Under the cover
Of the month's darkest night,
They loaded their weapons,
And prepared for the fight.

The chopper descended,
Ten miles from the beach;
It dropped a black raft,
Men slid into seats.

The motor then started,
They moved toward the land.
All of the fighters
With rifles in hand.

A mile out from shore
The boat stopped in the sea.
One final gear check,
Then a swim to the beach.

Once reality hit them
That they had reached sand,
They snatched up the gear
And hauled ass to dense land.

From there the team split
They each had an hour,
To get their jobs done,
And call command tower.

Each fighter moved quickly,
His friend was the night.
The waterproof face-paint
Helped stay out of sight.

All of a sudden
It came into view;
"The target's acquired,
Let's do what we do."

One reached for a sidearm
And opened the door.

Inside the straw hut
Was a family of four.

The man was the target.
So silent and still,
One looked down the pistol
And prepared for the kill.

But then, the infant
Asleep by the door,
Rolled off of its sleep mat
And onto the floor.

As it started to cry
On that still, perfect night
One turned around quickly,
And put out its lights.

The quiet, recovered
One slowly spun round.
The baby went quickly,
Without even a sound.

One looked at the father
Who had not even stirred.
Put three in his forehead
And shot his pet bird.

Out of the straw hut
So slowly One left;
He holstered the sidearm
And to the beach, crept.

His comrades were waiting
In the edge of the trees.
The call went to command post,
"Get us out of here please!"

Under cover of midnight
They swam out to the raft.
"Our mission's completed;
Let's get the Hell out!"

They started the engine,
A faint purr in the night.
They'd completed the mission
Without a firefight.

Some nightmares haunt men
From the things that they did;
Like putting two bullets
In an innocent kid.

There were no choices
When the infant did cry,
If the father had woken,
One might have died.

This is one small example
Of what the brave do,
In service and duty
Of the Red, White, and Blue.

About Mr. Jimmy

I met my friend, James Lodge, who I always called "Mr. Jimmy" when I began attending a new church in Alabama in 2014.

As adept as I consider myself to be at describing my feelings, intuitions, respect, admiration, and irritations; I just don't have the grammatical or literary prowess to articulate the amount of love, admiration, and respect that I cultivated for this man in the last years of his life.

Mr. Jimmy treated me better than my grandfather. He was more encouraging and more present at that particular time in my life than my own father was.

Through the years, when I wasn't traveling and I had the benefit of working locally, we had breakfast together at Bojangles in the mornings several days a week. Then, I would go to his home and we'd have coffee and Little Debbie cakes, he called them "sweet cakes", on my lunch hour.

He was as tough as a pine knot, and built like a spark plug with a personality to match. He was the physical epitome of "dynamite comes in small packages."

Mr. Jimmy was a warrior. He had beaten alcoholism, survived two branches of military service, raised two daughters and countless dogs, survived growing up in America with an abusive father who had been through the Great Depression and was as tough on Jimmy as Jimmy was on himself.

One day, during a visit to his home on my lunch break, as we were having our usual coffee and "sweet cakes", Mr. Jimmy looked at me with an innocent seriousness that I had never seen before. He had been having some health problems as of late, and I think he knew the end was drawing near.

"Adam", he said to me, "I need to ask you something."

"Sure. What's on your mind, buddy?" I replied.

"One day, I'm going to be leaving this place…. And, I was wondering… if you'd get up and say a few words…a few words about me…at my funeral…?"

"Mr. Jimmy," I told him, "I don't know if I can…. That's going to be hard day for me, when it comes…. But if it's important to you that I speak for you, … I'll do it."

"Thank, … Thank you, Adam…" he said to me, his voice trailing off.

That conversation was about a year and a half before he died.

I came to realize later on, that out of all the versions of himself that other people knew; it was me who knew the version of himself that he was most proud of. He wanted me to speak for him because of that one simple reason. He had lived into his seventies, and passed at age 76, one year longer than his father, who passed at age 75.

When he passed away on January 3, 2019, his daughters had to call me to get the information for his affairs, in order to take care of his funeral arrangements.

I have no doubt that God put James Lodge in my life to help me get through some of the tough times when I needed a coach in my corner. I just wish he could have stayed longer. I'm writing this book in 2026, and I still miss him every day.

I wrote the following poem the day after he passed away, and as he requested, I spoke at his funeral on January 7, 2019. Following a few thoughts, I read this poem to the attendees at his service. His oldest daughter published it on the back of his funeral card, so everyone that wanted one could have a copy.

I was honored to speak for my dear friend.

James "Mr. Jimmy" Lodge

When I met him, he was older,
He'd lived hard for many years;
A veteran, a pipefitter,
A man of little fear.

Though he was short in stature,
He was huge on the inside;
He was glad to be a Veteran,
It was a title held with pride.

We were kindred spirits right away,
Though many years apart,
But firmly grounded in the beliefs
We held in each our hearts.

Each day at lunch we'd visit,
Over coffee and "sweet cakes",
Often, we'd ponder politics,
Other times confess mistakes.

Sometimes a special trip we'd scheme
To get us out of town,
We'd have to get a biscuit
On the way to bust some rounds.

We'd shoot our guns and tell some jokes,
We discussed it all it seems,
I only wish for one more day,
Of memories like these.

I tried for one more visit,
Just this past Christmas Eve;
But my weary friend, he wasn't home,
Maybe it wasn't meant to be.

The last time that I saw him,
We joked about his "baby bump",
We talked about his family,
And the people that he loved.

As I left, I said, "I love you buddy"
And he replied the same,

My mentor, and my confidant,
He was so wise to life's games.

He told me he was proud of me,
And he thought of me, as a son,
"Always remember what I've said,
Your life's only just begun."

The greatest gift he gave me,
I'll cherish to my life's end,
Above our faith and kindredness,
Mr. Jimmy, was my friend.

What's In a Name

A friend of mine adopted a blue-nosed pit bull and her sister in 2011. The runt of the litter was named Angel, and he gifted her to me and my wife during a time when there were a lot of break-ins in our immediate area, even though we lived in the good part of Huntsville, Alabama.

I loved Angel, and she took to me right away. She was skittish at first because she came from an environment where there were nine children and lots of other dogs. Eventually, she came into her own and let her personality, love and loyalty shine like a diamond in our lives. She learned three languages, and was registered as a service dog for me, and became an integral part of our little family. She died just as she lived: with stoicism and grace.

Angel passed away of congestive heart failure on February 10, 2021. Her loss was devastating to our whole family. I had her cremated and I wear her ashes in a cross urn around my neck. That way, she can stay as close to my heart in death as she was in life.

I have never been able to get another dog, because I know there can only be one Angel for me.

She showed me the one thing that no human being has ever been able to; including my mother or either of my two former wives. On this earth, I've only known unconditional love from one source, and that was her.

Rest In Peace, my beautiful Angel.

What's In a Name

She was barely six weeks old;
On the ride home she got sick.
I gave her a third bath that day
And checked her good for ticks.

Her given name was Angel
But little did we know,
All the gifts this little girl
On our lives would bestow.

She was our protector,
Our other dog, too old.
Our Angel dog would have to
Watch our home, and do it bold.

She took well to her training,
Three languages she learned,
Thru patience, and thru loving,
Her total trust was earned.

I didn't know how much I needed her,
My soul was quite a mess,
She loved me unconditionally,
Even when I was not my best.

She'd give her life so willingly
If that's what the situation took,
She always paid attention
To others' energies, and looks.

One day she threw a Hella fit,
My wife questioned her with ire,
Then looking out the window,
Our neighbors' house had caught on fire!

She didn't know she was a hero,
Her story made the news.
They should have put her on the air;
It would've gotten tons of views.

Our heroine grew older,
She put on a little weight.

We didn't know her heart was failing
Until it was far too late.

A week and a half later,
On a trip back to the vet,
We had to tell our Angel bye,
Our hardest moment yet.

She lived her life for both of us;
So stoic and full of grace,
Our hearts have been forever changed;
Nothing could take her place.

It's been two years of healing;
I think about her every day,
But in the end, I know
Why God sent this Angel our way.

Rivers of Life

Even though I grew up in north Alabama, fishing the Tennessee River and other smaller rivers, lakes and ponds; none of them had the impact on me that the Yuba River in northern California or the Conejos River in Colorado have had.

I was very blessed to be able to visit Grass Valley California and help my younger brother move to Alabama in June of 2017. While there visiting, my brother wanted to make one last visit to his favorite place, the Yuba River. He had spoken many times prior about the energy at this special place that he loved so dearly, but I had no idea until I was able to visit it myself, with my brother and my father that summer.

I had an abrupt awakening, a profound spiritual experience there, which I am not prepared to divulge here, but I will say that if I ever get another chance to go back, I will do so without hesitation. The Yuba River is the only reason I would ever go back to California.

When I purchased my small ranch in Colorado, I knew nothing of the area besides the small river that runs near my ranch. However, as I got to learn the area and began later to work with the Amish, I discovered the Conejos River. Conejos means "Rabbit" in Spanish and also in some of the local Native American tribal language.

The Conejos River has a very special energy in its life force. I visit it every time I travel to Colorado and I always feel a special kind of cleansing afterwards. The last time I went to visit, my therapist had given me instructions on how to pray for forgiveness and to release any anger or bitterness or hurt and shame that I felt like others had laden me with. I took his step-by-step instructions with me on the trip and followed them word for word while in the Conejos River. I honestly felt like a new person afterwards.

Perhaps it's because I am a Taurus and I've always been drawn to the woods and the water, or perhaps it's some other reason unbeknownst to me that the wild has always soothed my soul. Regardless of what it is, I am grateful.

Rivers of Life

The Yuba and Conejos,
Two rivers that I love.
The energy within them
Originates from far above.

The glacier melt that feeds them
Frigid on the hottest days,
Has the power in its life force
To clear the cluttered mind of haze.

And clarity is nourishment
For the weary, heavy soul,
Who visits in the moments
Life has taken quite a toll.

Within the rushing waters
Healing energy abounds,
To give to those who seek it
The answers they need found.

Sometimes it's not an answer
That the heavy soul doth seek.
Sometimes the weary traveler,
Longs to hear the water speak.

Whether on the shore in silence,
Or fly-fishing with dear friends,
The river serves a purpose,
For troubled souls to mend.

Either rushing or in ripples
The river never minds to play;
The waters just seem happy
That someone visited today.

The Water and The Woodlands

There is something about the water and the woods that has always drawn me to them.

I have a picture of me as a little boy when I caught my very first fish. My dad took me to a pond out in a field behind the house we were renting, rigged us each up a cane pole and when I hooked that first little Bluegill, fishing hooked me! I don't know if it was the magic and the mystery of the experience to my little boy mind, or maybe it was the thought that if my dad could do this thing that makes fish get on this hook, maybe I could do it too.

Dad and I walked back to the little white farm house, and my mother took a picture of us with the fish, and then she took one of just me holding the line up, the fish hanging from the hook as still as could be, even though it was still alive. I think we took it back to the pond and let it go after the celebration. I know we didn't eat it, either, but we sure ate a lot of fish and had a lot of family fish fries through the years later.

As a young man, I took up backpacking in Bankhead Forest in North Alabama. I loved going to one particular spot where there was a waterfall and I'd camp on top of it with my backpacking buddy for a week at a time.

Later in life, when I found myself at a crossroads, not knowing what to do or where to turn, but knowing a major decision had to be made, and it was solely up to me to decide which direction my life would take; I would always find myself on top of that same waterfall; sitting on a fallen tree, hanging out over the edge, searching my heart and soul for the logical answer with the roar of the descending water cascading over the edge of the rock face and crashing into the rocks fifty feet below.

As time has passed, I have relocated and traveled much across these United States. In recent years I have found myself pondering these decisions at the Yuba River in northern California, and most recently, at the Conejos River in southern Colorado. Just as time moves forward and the decisions become more important, we must continue to move forward to new locations, and with people different from those we leave behind.

In September of 2025, while on a spur-of-the-moment trip to Colorado, I found myself making a trip to the Conejos River. I was going to a special place, a campground, called Aspen Glade that I hadn't been to in two and a half years. The camping season was coming to a close and I remembered that the state usually closed Aspen Glade around Labor Day and wouldn't reopen until spring.

I had been visiting an Amish friend who lived about a half an hour from this special place so I decided to go and soak up some of the last of the available time there before the state locked the gate for the season. My truck was silent aside from the rumbling of the diesel engine, and the windows were down. Out the driver's side window, the landscape was changing from fields of livestock to rolling mountain hills. As I drove further toward the mountain pass, the hills began to steepen and there were incredibly straight, beautiful Aspen trees; all lined up like soldiers in rows going straight up to the tops of those mountains. The mountain hills began to converge with each other like ocean waves of green Aspens and evergreen pines with huge boulders interspersed throughout the landscape. The smell of sage and pine and the clean water of the Conejos River running through the canyon at the base of these mountains was flowing through the cab of my truck with all the windows down.

It was just me, and the road, and the wind, and the water, and the smell of the Rocky Mountains; the hum of the engine and whistle of the turbo; the sound of my tires on the asphalt. I noticed my face was starting to hurt for some reason. I didn't feel like anything was wrong with me medically, but just in case I looked into the rear-view mirror. There I found my answer. I had been smiling so big, and so hard, for so long, that my cheeks were sore. I don't remember the last time I had been so happy that my face hurt. It seems like only yesterday I left, and I look forward to going back again. It can't happen soon enough.

I hope you find in your life, a special place to make critical decisions that provide you the type of peace and solitude necessary to move forward with purpose, peace, and confidence.

The Water & the Woodlands

Ever since I can remember,
From the side of the pond with Dad;
To the day that I surrendered
The only wife I'd ever had.

From all the days of boyhood
Now many years a man,
The water and the woodlands
Have never dropped my hand.

I went to them in good times
In my youth with many friends.
I found solitude in hard times,
But the courage to start again.

They've never given up on me,
And I've been faithful to them too,
The water and the woodlands
Are there, to help to get me thru.

From the worst life has to offer,
To the joyous times of bliss
The water and the woodlands
When I leave earth, I will miss.

I wrote this poem in Colorado, while working with the Amish. We were building a beautiful log cabin nestled in the Rockies and I was contemplating life one day on a lunch break.

There is something so beautiful and so special about the energy in Colorado that has a tendency to pull the words out of me and inspires me to effortlessly organize them on the page. I wish I had a better way to explain it, but it just happens that way. Writing became an incredible therapy for me in those mountains and during those months of transforming and reclaiming my life, and in a lot of ways, coming full circle back to the old me. I'm looking forward to being back in Colorado again, permanently, someday.

Lessons

We come into this earthly realm
Thru birth, we're given life.
That moment when we first arrive,
We know nothing of strife.

Time ticks by for each of us,
Then we begin to walk.
Our loved ones seem unable
To wait to hear our baby talk.

Our Infancy now behind us,
Adolescence looms ahead;
Playing sports and school work
Occupies our time instead.

We begin to take up challenges
And come into our own,
The teenage years appear at once
At times, we seek to be alone.

Through all the years along our path
There are battles we must fight.
Sometimes the scars those battles leave
Make for a restless night.

The warrior within us all
Gets better day by day,
While the battles that we failed to win,
Haunt our soul in every way.

Adulthood brings new challenges
More battles will ensue,
It's up to us to fight them fiercely,
And if not us, then who?

The inner warrior rallies,
By now, we're scarred and strong;
With any luck we'll have comrades,
To push and keep us moving on.

The warrior mentality,
Our Society detests,

But through the battle scars we earn,
We learn our lessons best.

About My Life Coach

I was referred to my life coach, by my EPT therapist, Kim Dillon, in Alabama that I had been working with for an extended period of time. I remember the very day that I called her. My laptop had crashed, and my wife was driving me to the Decatur, Alabama Office Depot for one last attempt at recovering my hard drive. (The hard drive was unrecoverable.) That computer had more than twenty years of my life on it.

In recent weeks prior, my service dog, Angel, had passed away leaving me devastated and completely lost. Prior to that, my business had caught fire and I lost my entire livelihood, my life savings, and myself. Even though I had tried to go back into business, due to the Covid pandemic, the state of Alabama had shut me down when I bought a food trailer, then the food trailer had been destroyed in a violent tornado a year after I had bought it. It was as if Satan himself had latched on to me and refused to let go.

As we were driving down the highway, I sat in the passenger's seat and I told my wife, that I had seen a hypnotherapist on a show I'd been watching and I wanted to seek help from one, but everyone that I had called and left messages with, had produced no results and I was at my wit's end. I just didn't know what else I could do. That's when she suggested I call Kim. "Maybe she knows someone.", she had said hopefully.

I called Kim immediately and it just happened that she had a friend who had used a hypnotist to help her quit smoking and it actually worked! I begged for the number, and she said she'd get back to me.

It was later that afternoon that a man called me. His name is Yorbe Caoba. It turned out that he was an Atheist, and I had turned agnostic for a period of time in the past. His spirituality didn't make a difference to me. I needed help, and he was there. He lived in north Alabama as well, and after we talked that first time, he was willing to help me. And that's how my healing journey began. One call at a time.

The poem below is our story. Sadly, we have lost contact since both of us got divorces, moved out of Alabama, and changed phone numbers; but

I will always be grateful for him and everything he helped me through.

My Life Coach

God sent to me an Atheist,
But we wouldn't meet for a year.
It was always the logistics,
And never about a fear.

We used today's technology,
Our calls were each about an hour.
But every time we tried to meet,
Something would make it sour.

And so it was, just chatting,
Confessing to him just like a priest,
And the entire time, the knowing
I was never judged in the least.

This time for me was daunting,
I found him at my worst.
He had the patience that I needed,
More practicality, at first.

I started setting daily goals,
And celebrating little wins.
I was starting over at the bottom,
With my wife, and fewer friends.

The baby steps continued;
The wins started to get bigger.
I was moving forward with a purpose;
My emotions were less triggered.

I followed more of his instructions;
And I strove hard to forgive.
By letting go and embracing loss,
I was letting myself live.

Now, a healing warrior,
My strength was coming back.
I decided on a direction,
And mounted my attack.

I achieved a major life goal
And became a teacher for six months,

Then the planets got together,
And gave me a gut punch.

But the fighter within me rallied,
Another time for change was nigh,
It was a move to Colorado;
Another lifelong dream of mine.

Before I left, we met one time.
It was one in person session,
And with our work completed,
I had one last confession.

I profusely thanked him
For how far I had come,
And let him know that he changed my life
In a big way, not just "some".

When I arrived in Colorado,
He was the very first to say
"Welcome Home now, Adam.
Your new life begins today."

From practicality to wisdom,
And ever so much more,
This Atheist, my life coach;
I can't help but adore.

Our time had come for parting,
He told me one day on a call.
But afterwards an accident,
Had him staring at four walls.

He was lucky to be alive,
He had broken many bones,
He wasn't able to conversate,
Or even use his phone.

His recovery has been grueling,
But the advice he gave me stands,
He'd kept moving forward too,
While recovering; he'd made plans.

He's helped me in so many ways
I can't reiterate enough,
When I was at my weakest
He showed me I was tough.

He's never given up on me,
Ever thankful will I stay,
The Atheist God sent me,
Helped make me who I am today.

I remember the doctor's appointment vividly. It was exactly ninety days after my 40th birthday, also a Friday the 13th when I got the news.

"You know you're diabetic, right?" the doctor made more of a statement than a question.

"No. I didn't know that." I told him.

The exchange changed everything for me. I was now at place in my life where my worst fear was a reality.

"I'm going to beat this." I told him; and I meant it. And I did it in less than a year post diagnosis.

My life was falling apart. I had taken on a life coach in the months prior to this day. He had been working with me, encouraging me, and helping me to find my way. I felt so lucky and blessed to have him. The one thing that still sticks in my mind to this day, is what he said to me during our very first conversation. I had poured out my soul to him.

I had told him everything that had happened in my life since 2017 and most of it was horrific. It was like my life was in a downward spiral that I couldn't escape. I was at a place where it seemed that I dealt with nothing but constant loss. I felt like the world was closing in on me and there was nowhere to run, and nowhere to hide. Even though I was a fighter, I was weary of the battles that seemed to be wave after wave of onslaught from an enemy that I could not see or engage. How do you fight something you can't see?

At the end of that first conversation with the life coach, he said to me, "Adam, I'm going to be honest. Most people in your situation wouldn't be able to deal with everything you've been going thru these last few years. They wouldn't even be here anymore. Most people, had they been put in your shoes, would have given up. That tells me exactly how strong you are and how resilient you've had to be to endure all this. I really want to help you."

"Thank God. You were my last hope.", I told him. I honestly didn't have anywhere else to turn. I had already tapped into all my resources and exhausted all of my network, except for my friend, Kim, who had referred me to him. That first conversation was when the work began.

Fast forward about a year and we had made excellent progress, but this time, I was now diagnosed with Type 2 Diabetes. The medication was wrecking my life. I had just spent two months moving out of a house and into an apartment; and due to the move, I had been forced to quit a job I loved and was extremely good at.

This time, I was again on the phone with the life coach. I needed to be needed and I needed to be busy. I love to work and not doing so was slowly killing me just like the diabetes medication seemed to be.

"How long has it been since you tapped into your network in Colorado?", he asked me on the phone that day.

"Over a year." I told him. I couldn't believe it had been that long, but it was true. I dearly missed Colorado.

"Call them all, and see if anyone has any job leads. It never hurts to ask, and you might be surprised at what could come up for you.", he said.

"I'll call them now. Maybe you're right. I guess it's worth a shot. I'm really out of options at this point.", I told him.

I made two phone calls, and the second one changed everything.

My friend's girlfriend was in a long-term care facility in Denver with "Long Covid". His two current ranch hands were burnt out and had given their resignation. He was staying with his daughter in Colorado Springs in order to visit his love daily in Denver. He needed someone to live on, and care for, his ranch and his livestock. I had been longing for Colorado. My heart had been aching to be back as soon as I had to leave the last time. It was finally time for me to return to the one place that felt like home.

This poem is about that period in my life. It was more or less a late "Vision Quest" that I desperately needed.

When I left for Colorado, I had lost almost everything in my life. Literally. My business, my service dog, both grandparents, my laptop and over twenty years of memories and writing projects, partially written books, all of my memories with my wife of eleven years including all of our wedding photos and videos. So much of my life was gone; never to be recovered, and that's just the tip of the iceberg.

I do not know what would have happened or where I would be today if I had not taken the opportunity to go live and work in Colorado for that period of time. I'm supremely grateful to have had the chance to work through my mental load and clear my soul, as well as to have had all the new experiences that I was blessed with during those months. It was completely refreshing to have so many wins and turn the tide in my life.

I hope you enjoy "A Year of Change" and I encourage you to take your own "Vision Quest" in life, if you ever have the need. The growth you experience, and the change in your perspective will be more rewarding than anything you ever thought possible. It's never too late, as long as you're breathing.

A Year of Change

A year in Colorado,
The time has gone by fast.
I've done so much and come so far,
I'm better than my past.

It started with a favor
To help a loving friend.
I came to run a private ranch,
And did so, till the end.

Then winds of change arrived
With the summer just beginning;
I started working with the Amish,
Then achieved my "patent pending"!

Building cabins in the Rockies
Had been a secret dream of mine.
The claims that held my "office views"
Were untouched by sands of time.

An unforgettable experience
Describes my first elk hunt!
On our way out, a jagged rock
Sliced the driver's tire in front!

Four Amish and one English,
One driver's steer tire down,
It took less than an hour
To be back on the road to town.

There's much more to the story!
In this year, I wrote a book;
I've almost finished editing,
And designed the cover look.

I've undergone hypnosis
To conquer underlying fears;
Again, I'm writing poetry;
I've not done so in years.

I cured my diabetes
And I've started copywriting;

Now building an online business;
In Colorado I am thriving!

This year has not been easy.
It's been challenging at best;
The old me would have made it
But the new me aced this test.

My uncle Rodney was my mother's brother. He was one of a pair of identical twins. He was truly a cowboy, even though he worked at Delphi (General Motors) in Athens, Alabama. He raised horses on his 50-acre farm, got his son involved in barrel racing, shot guns, taught his sons and all of us nephews to shoot and gave us all pointers in the art of shooting. He had a pond full of fish, purchased dirt bikes, four-wheelers, tractors, and equipment for use on his farm. He had a huge metal shop where he and my cousins would rebuild engines, restore cars, and work on boats and all kinds of other projects. He had every tool imaginable. He was a country boy in every sense of the word. He was also a pilot, and everyone's favorite uncle. His smile and charisma were infectious.

A few years after his death, his white cowboy hat was gifted to me by his oldest son, along with a chocolate brown and a forest green one.

After my cousin bought his own house in Southerland Springs, Texas, as I was leaving from visiting, I left the hat on display in the China Cabinet. I still have the chocolate brown cowboy hat, but it just felt right to leave the white one with his oldest son. I'm finished with my traveling days as an entrepreneurial business coach. I'm just glad that Uncle Rodney was along for the ride with me for a time.

Rodney's Cowboy Hat

My uncle Rodney had a cowboy hat
He wore when he would drive to church.
He pulled up in his red Cadillac
And on his head, it perched.

He'd sit it on the leather dash
And then he would stroll inside;
The hat was made by Justin,
White, and the brim was curled and wide.

Sometimes he wore it as he traveled,
To impact meetings for Al-Anon;
Then it rested on his closet shelf
After Rodney's peace, he'd won.

Gifted to me by my cousin,
His first and eldest boy,
I began to wear it in my travels,
And it truly brought me joy.

Uncle Rodney had a lot of smarts,
He was more than a maintenance man;
He had traveled for robotics
Classes all across the land.

Sometimes, the hat would make the trips
And other times stay home;
His hat has been my comfort,
Out here on the road alone.

Though Rodney's gone; his hat remains;
I wear it in my travels now.
And though I'm smart,
My little head can't fill it anyhow.

But nonetheless, I wear it still;
I never drive alone.
Because Rodney's always with me,
On the road to my next "home".